What A ?

By Anne Giulieri

I am little.

I am brown and yellow.

I like to fly.

Look at me.

What am I?

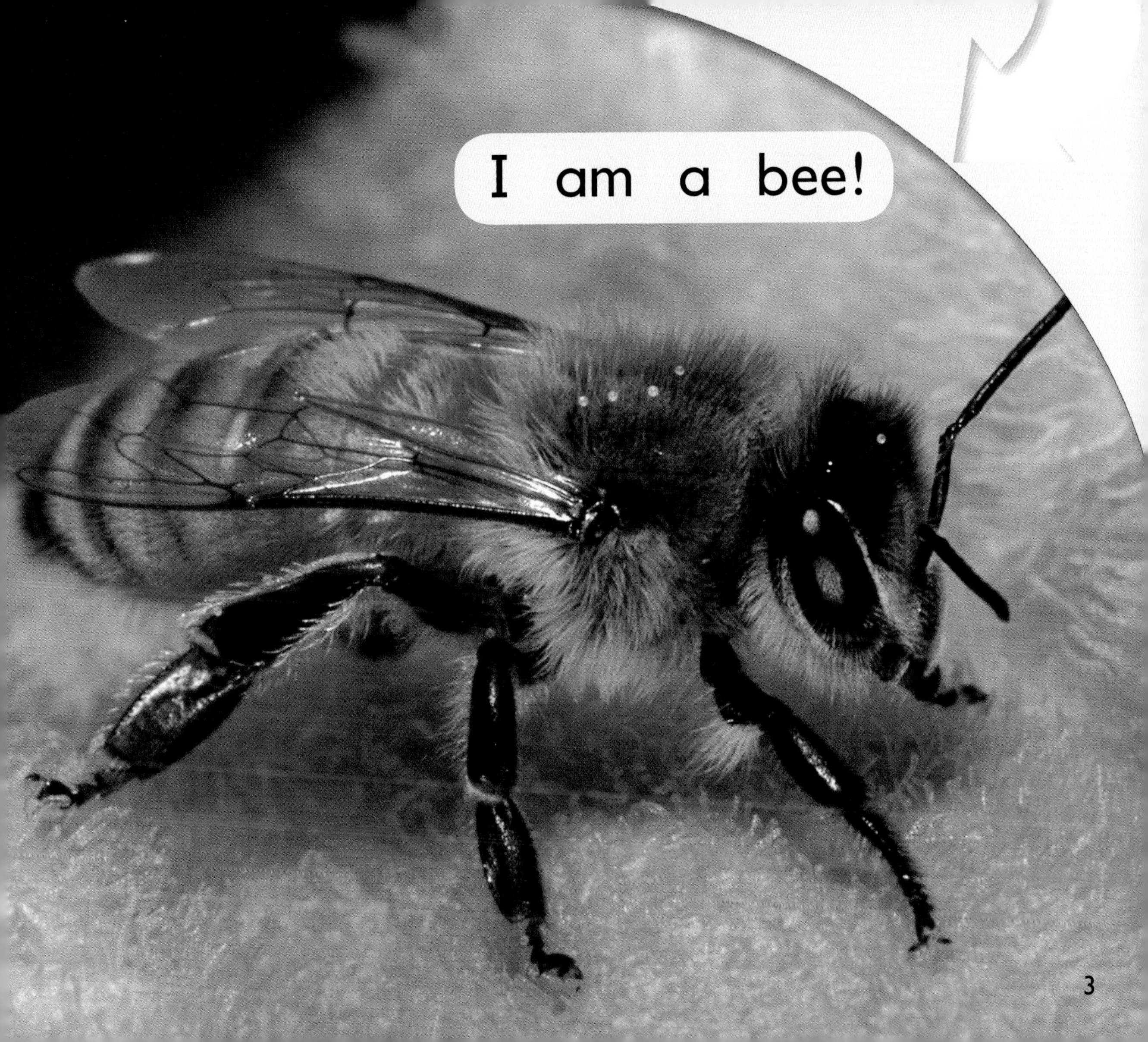

I am a bee!

I am little.

I am blue.

I like to fly.

Look at me.

What am I?

I am a butterfly!

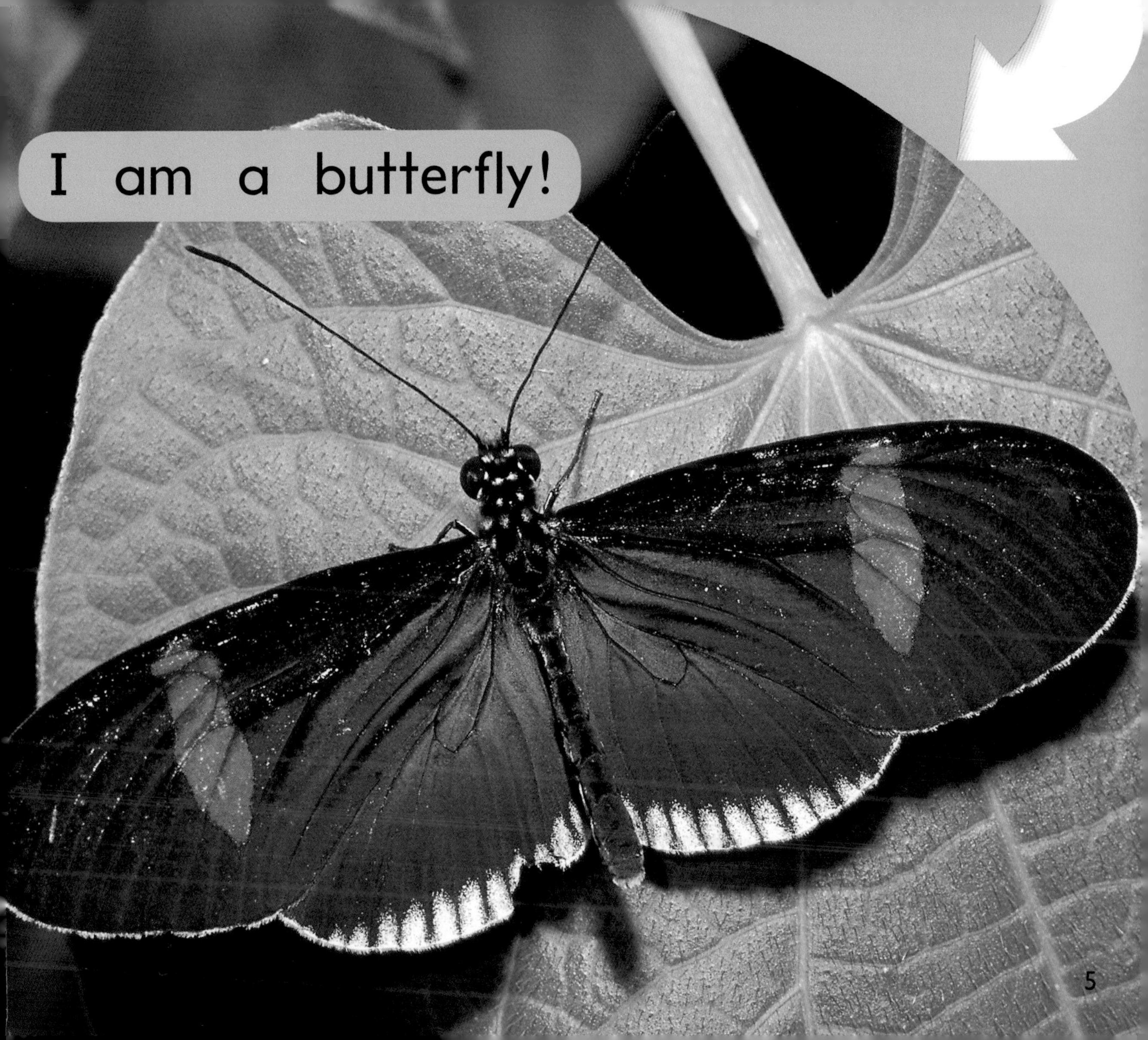

I am little.

I am brown.

I like to fly.

Look at me.

What am I?

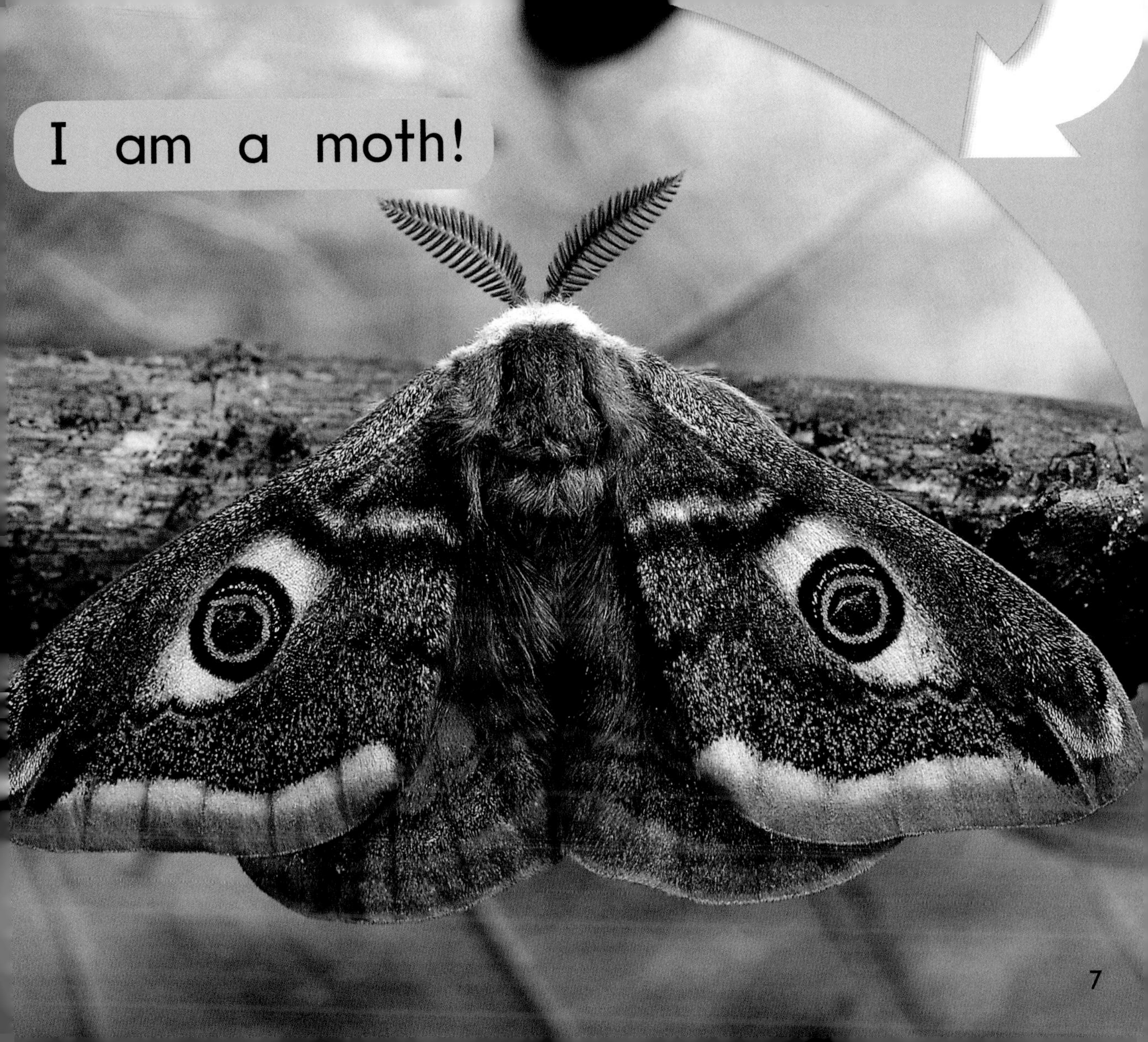

I am a moth!

I am little.

I am red and black.

I like to fly.

Look at me.

What am I?

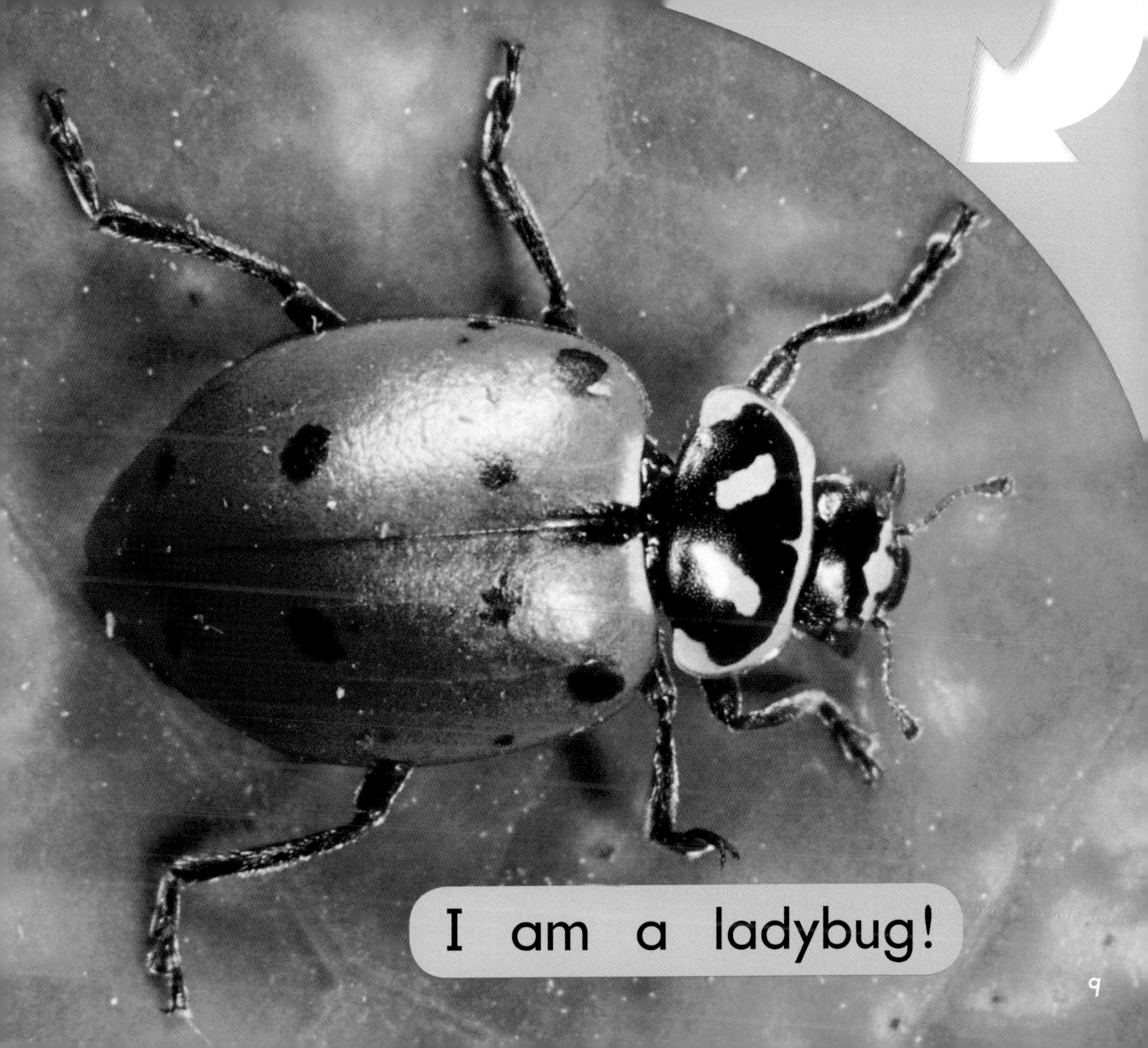

I am a ladybug!

I am little.

I am brown and black.

I like to fly.

Look at me.

What am I?

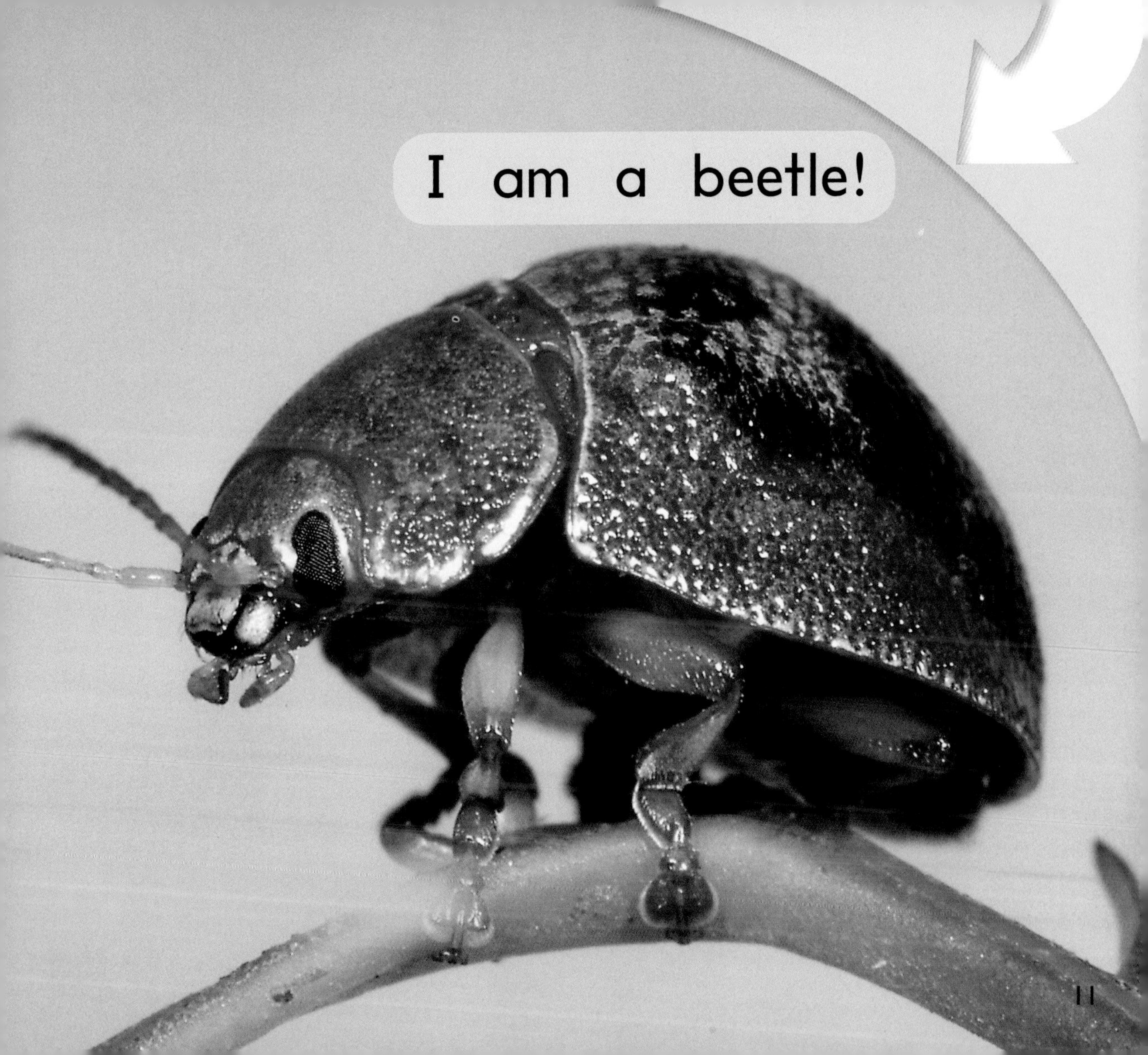

I am a beetle!

I am little.

I am black.

I like to fly.

Look at me.

What am I?

I am a dragonfly!

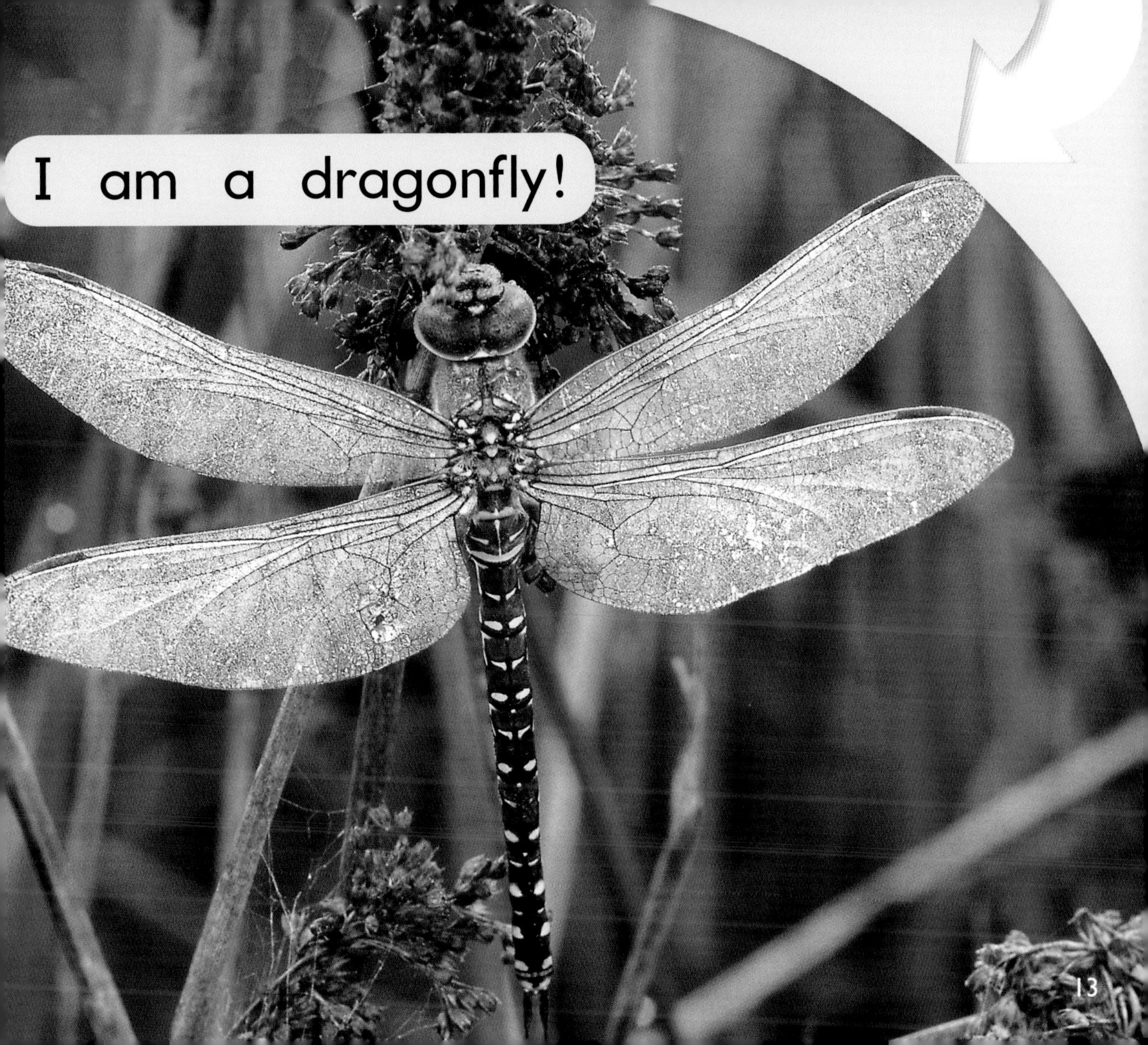

I am little.

I am black.

I like to fly.

Look at me.

What am I?

I am a mosquito!

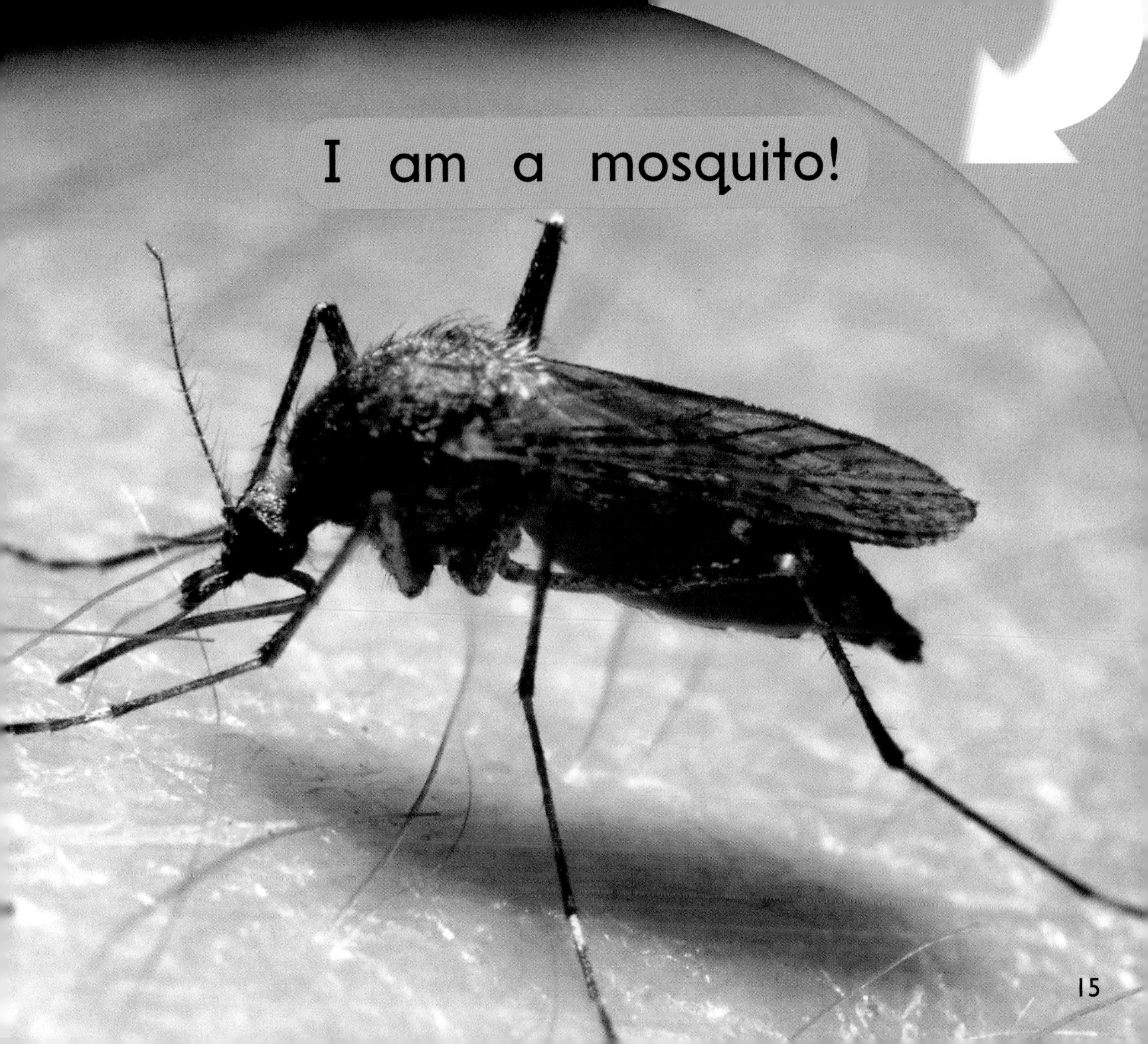

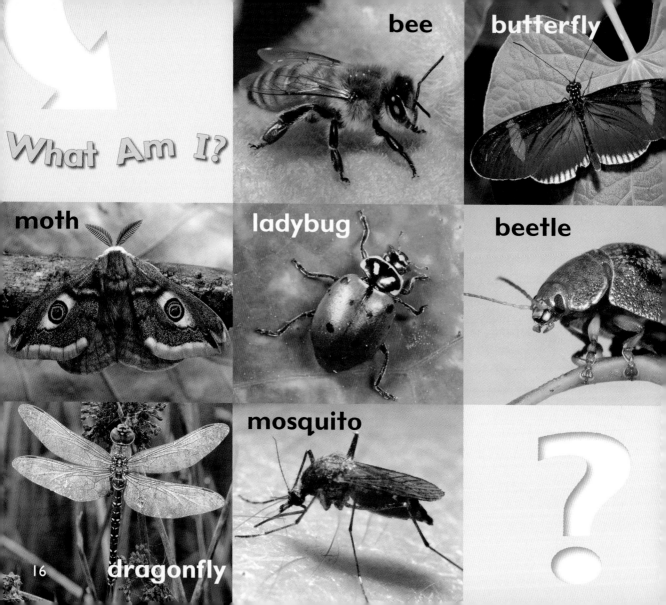

What Am I?

bee

butterfly

moth

ladybug

beetle

dragonfly

mosquito

?

16